The Little Brain

JYOTI MISHRA

ILLUSTRATIONS BY GRACE WIGUNA

First Edition

Fulton Books
Meadville, PA

Published by Fulton Books 2022

ISBN 979-8-88505-418-8 (paperback)
ISBN 978-1-63985-855-2 (hardcover)
ISBN 978-1-63985-854-5 (digital)

Printed in the United States of America

For Ayan and Amaya, my little brains.

J.M.

Once upon a time, there was a little brain. He had big dreams! He wanted to play tennis like a famous athlete.

He wanted to act like a movie star. He wanted to sing the sweetest songs. And he wanted to write a delightful storybook.

He asked a brain scientist, “How do I do this?”

The scientist told him to play tennis every day, to act every day, to sing every day, and to write about all that he could imagine every single day.

The little brain did the things he loved to do again and again and again. The little brain was discovering the first secret of learning—*practice*.

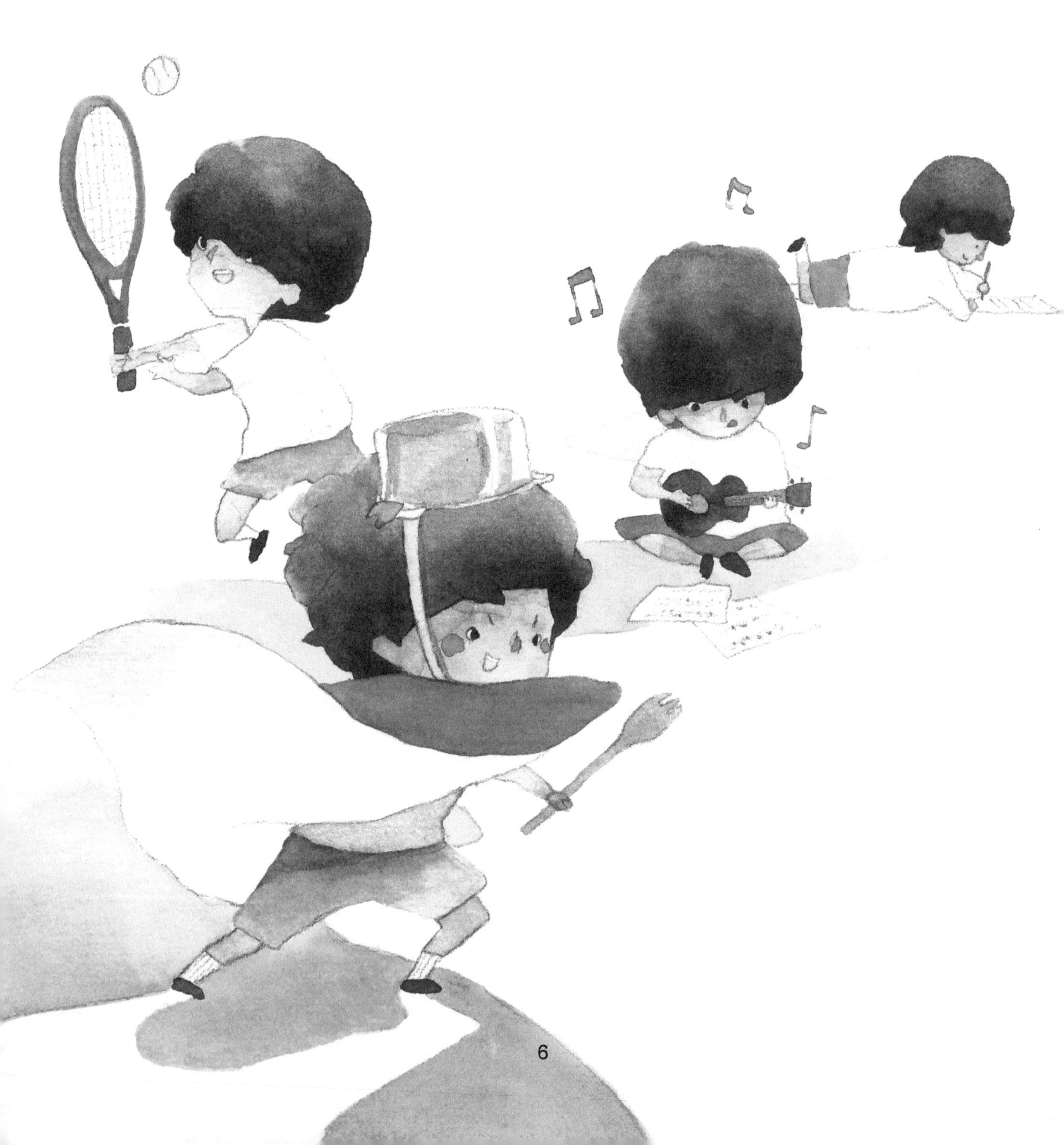

On some days, the little brain felt that he practiced well. On other days, he felt he could not learn at all.

So he went back to the scientist and asked her, "Why is this happening?"

The scientist said, "Little brain, you need the second secret of learning. And that is *focus*. *Focus* is when you hit the tennis ball as if you can only see the ball and nothing else around. *Focus* is when you act and sing without thinking about anyone watching or listening to you.

Focus is when you can imagine and write a story and not notice who else is in the room with you. When you have *focus*, there is nothing that can stop you from learning well!"

With *practice* and *focus* in his bag, the happy little brain could now learn very well. After some time, he could hit the ball hard every time.

He could really captivate the audience when he acted. He could sing a beautiful song in perfect tune. And he could write a story from his very own imagination.

So he went back to the scientist and asked, “Can you tell if I will now be the best tennis player or a movie superstar? Can you tell if I will now sing like a popstar or write a best-selling book?”

The scientist smiled. She said, “To be that good, I need to tell you the third secret of learning. And that is *challenge*.

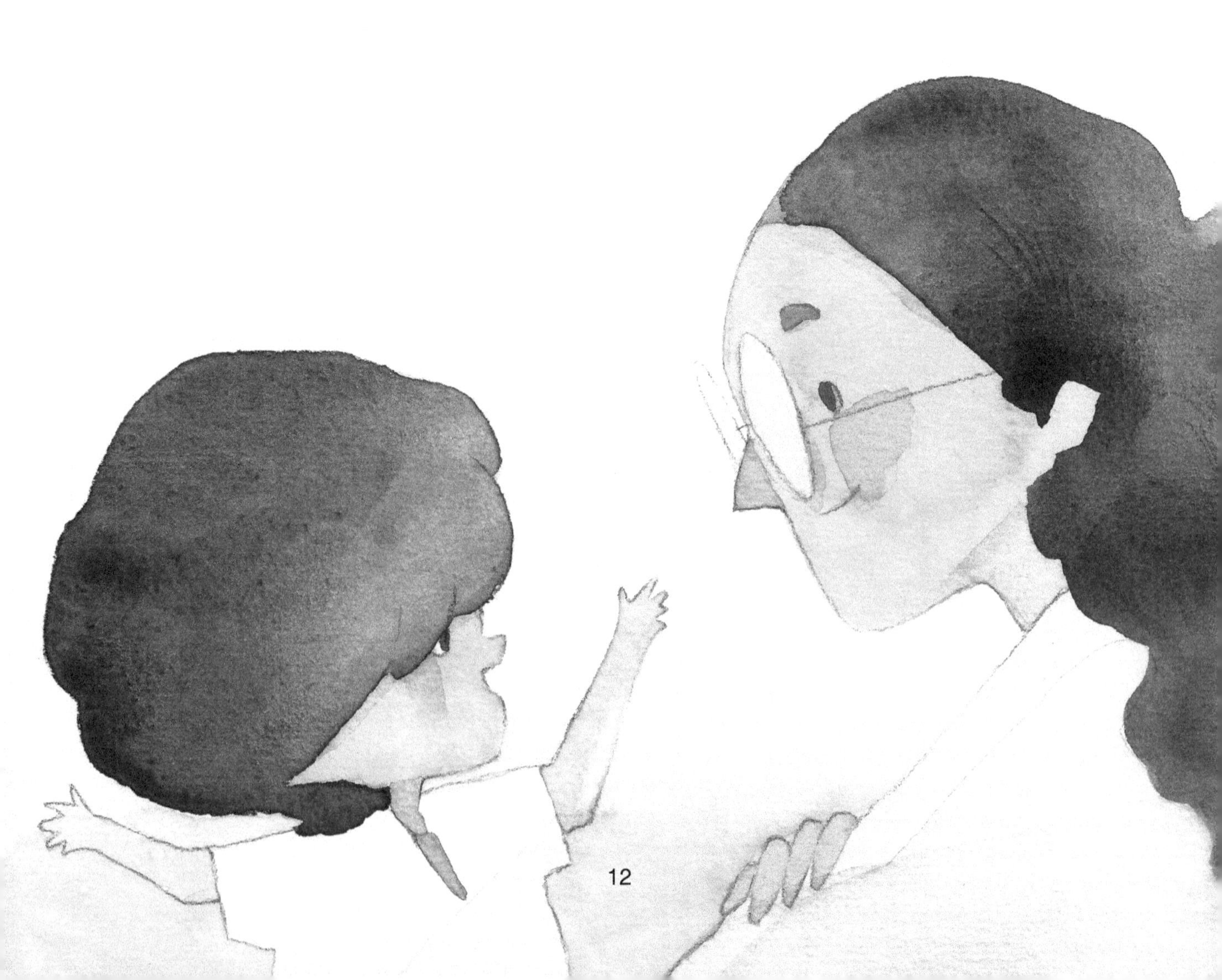

Challenge is a mountain that you want to climb. It has snow on it, so it is slippery. It has rocks on it, so you may trip. You will fall again and again on this mountain. But if you keep trying, you *will* reach the top."

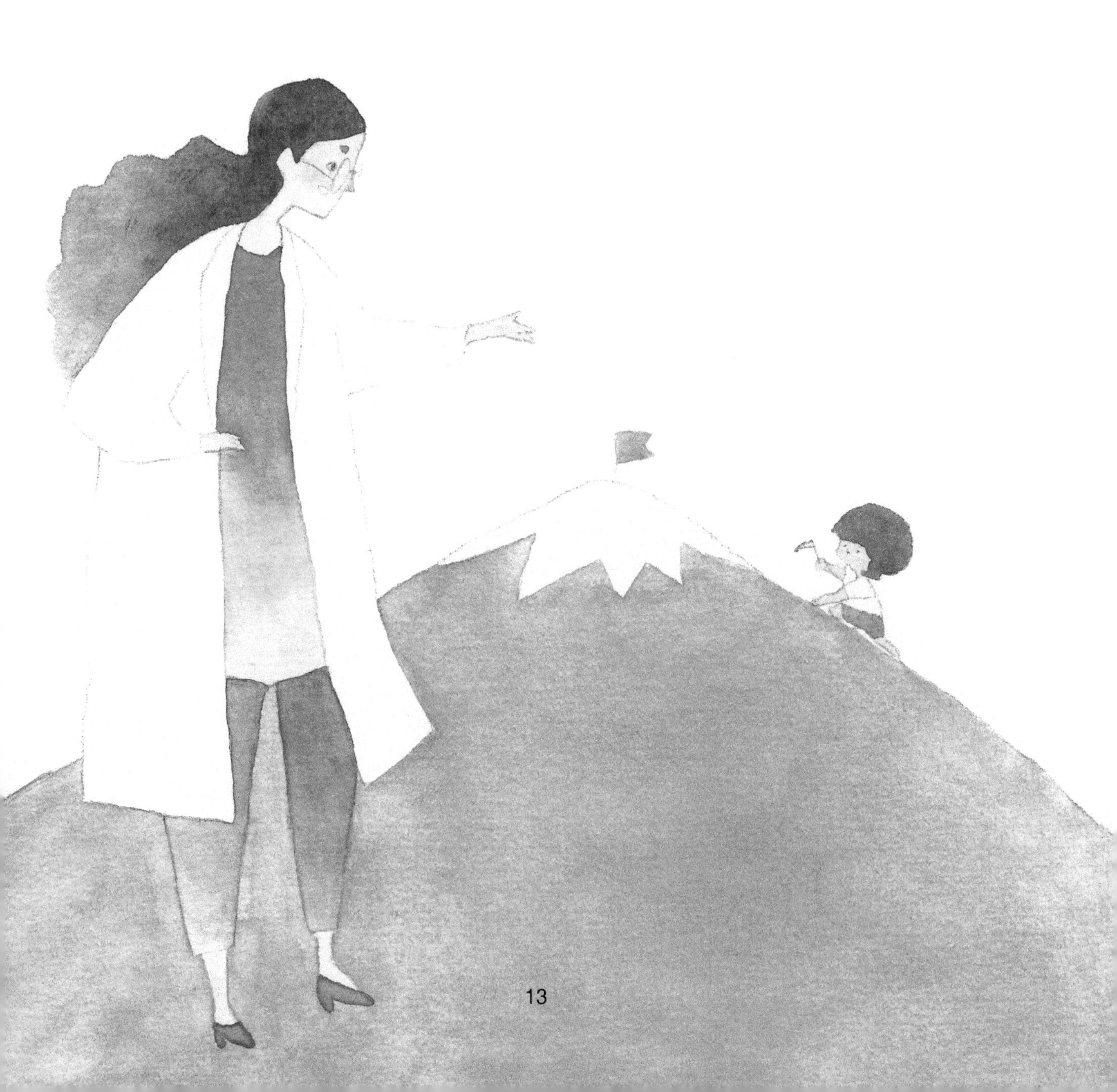

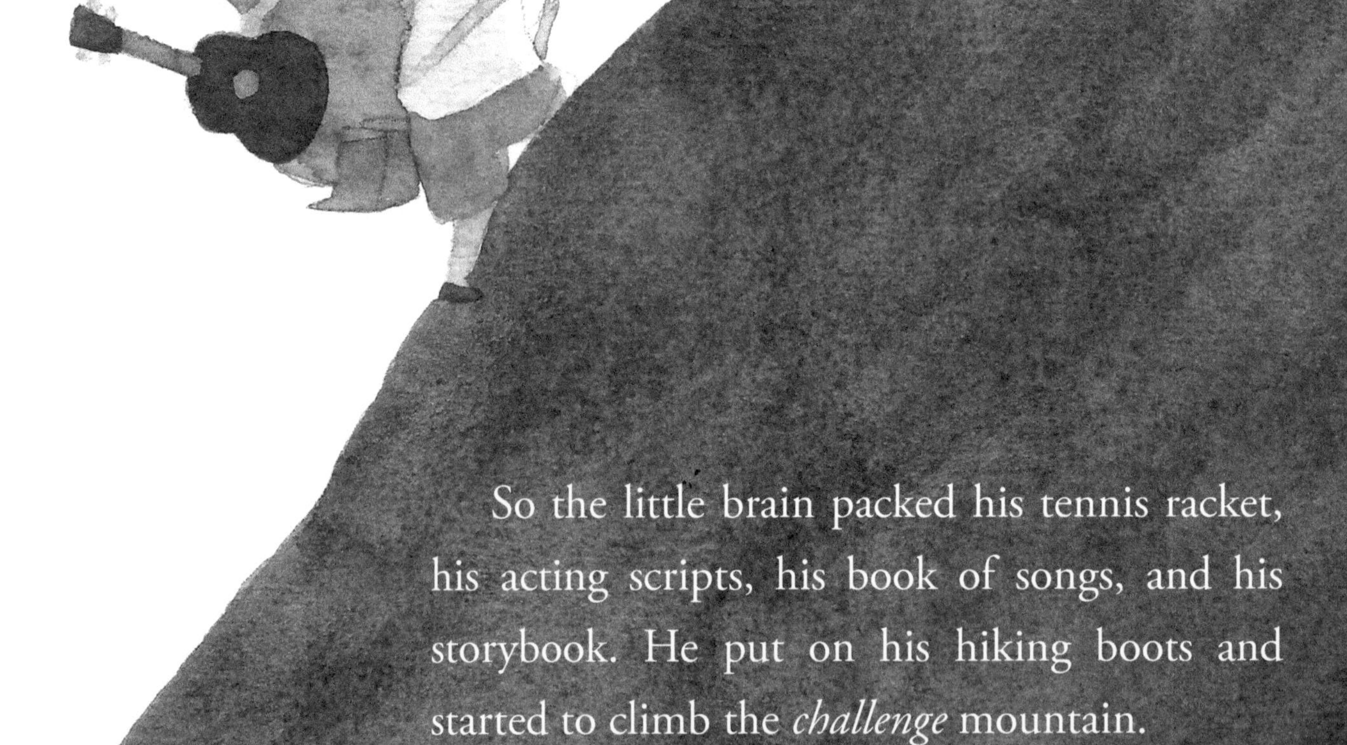

So the little brain packed his tennis racket, his acting scripts, his book of songs, and his storybook. He put on his hiking boots and started to climb the *challenge* mountain.

Indeed, it was a tricky mountain to climb. It took him many years to climb it.

On the way to the top, he got tired. He thought, *Oh! I'm not so good at this! I'm tired! I will never get to the peak!*

The little brain was not so little anymore. He thought about the scientist and called her on the phone.

The scientist was delighted to hear from him. "It's so good to hear from you, little brain, after so many years. It sounds like you are tired. But never give up! Take a deep breath and try to enjoy every slope on *challenge* mountain. I think it's time for me to give you the fourth secret of learning. And that is *grit*. *Grit* is the magic Band-Aid that you will use every time you fall on *challenge* mountain. It's okay to fall once, twice, or many times. Every time you do, just put on the magic Band-Aid and remember to say to yourself, 'I can do this if I try! I can do this even if I fall!'"

After some more years, with *practice*, *focus*, *challenge*, and *grit*, the not-so-little brain reached the peak. The little brain was now a big brain.

He was now a star actor.

He was now an expert athlete.

He was a pop singer.

And he could write stories that all the world wanted to read.

One day, he met the scientist again and said, “Thank you for teaching me so much! Do you think I am the best brain in the world?”

That day, the scientist gave him the very last secret of learning. She said, “Indeed, big brain, you have learned so much! Now you must do what all big brains do…and that is to *share* your learning with other little brains.

Always play together, sing together, and learn together.
That is how you become a better and better brain every day!"

About the Author

Jyoti Mishra is a brain scientist. She studies how our brains help us pay attention and learn throughout life. Being a scientist is her dream job! Jyoti lives in San Diego, California with her husband and two amazing children. Visit Jyoti at neatlabs.org

Grace Wiguna lives in Indonesia. She loves to make art with watercolors and teach it to little brains.

Lightning Source UK Ltd.
Milton Keynes UK
UKHW050629121122
412038UK00005B/131